ANGELMOUSE

An Important Message

by Rodney Peppé

"Breakfast's ready!"

Quilly had made a lovely meal.

But where was Angelmouse?

At last, he appeared. He sat down and put some sugar in his tea. Quilly knew what he was going to do next.

"Don't use your tail!"

But Angelmouse ignored him.

"Ow!" he squealed.

Just then, there was a rattling sound at the front door.

"Mail!" called Angelmouse. There was a piece of cloth stuck halfway through the mailbox. Angelmouse grabbed it and pulled it out.

"Oh, it's only an old blankety thing!" he said, throwing it on the floor.

"Stop!" cried Quilly. "It's from You-know-who! Look, there's a message. It says: **Please return the precious cloth to...**"

But the rest of the message had been torn off.

"It might be stuck in the mailbox," said Quilly.

The pair looked inside and outside, but they couldn't find the other half of the message anywhere.

"It's gone...blown away...never mind!" said Angelmouse. "It's only a boring old piece of blankety thing."

"But it's precious to **somebody**," Quilly reminded him. "And you've got to find out who."

Angelmouse scowled. Then his halo went wobbly.

Angelmouse and Quilly flew off to find the owner of the cloth. First, the friends visited Hutchkin.

"Hey, I'm like, busy, man," said Hutchkin. "I'm counting carrots."

But Angelmouse burst in anyway. "Is this yours?" he asked, holding up the cloth.

"No. Hey, watch my carrots, man!" Too late. The carrots were scattered everywhere. "Oh, no! I'll have to start counting all over again."

"Sorry," said Angelmouse.

"It's not his, Quilly," Angelmouse reported as Hutchkin pushed him out of his burrow.

"Let's try Spencer," suggested Quilly. "It might be his."

Angelmouse and Quilly flew high into the sky, with
Angelmouse wearing the cloth like a cape around his shoulders.
Then, suddenly, the cloth blew off!

"Oh, no!" The cloth floated down and down...

...and it landed on Spencer's car!

"Bucket, water, sponge, wax, squeegee, duster..." listed Spencer. "Where did I put that duster?"

Spencer noticed the cloth. "There! Duster. Cleaning kit all present and accounted for."

Just then, Angelmouse and
Quilly swooped down from the sky.

"So it's your cloth!" said Angelmouse.

"Not really a cloth. Just a bit of old rag I found,"
answered Spencer.

"It may be an old rag to you," said Angelmouse.
"But it's very precious to someone!"

Angelmouse took the cloth away from Spencer.

"It's Angelmouse's job to return the cloth to its owner," explained Quilly. "Any idea who it belongs to, Spencer?"

"Try Oswald. He's always losing things," said Spencer. "Look out! Here he comes!"

Oswald was speeding down
the street on his roller skates.

He was out of control!

"No brakes! No brakes!" he shouted.

Angelmouse waved the cloth
frantically at Oswald. "Is this yours?" he asked.

"Never seen it before! Never seen it before!" shouted Oswald. As he skated away, the wind caught the cloth and blew it into the park.

"Oh, no!" cried Angelmouse, and he and Quilly set off.

Angelmouse caught the cloth and sighed. "I'll never find the person who's lost this precious cloth. I give up! I'm going home."

His halo began to wobble wildly. Quilly pointed to it and said, "You-know-who won't be very pleased."

"Don't care," pouted Angelmouse. Pop! His halo vanished.

At that moment, Elliemum walked by with Baby Ellie.

"Hello, Elliemum," Angelmouse called. "How are you?"

"Me? I'm as fit as a fiddle," said Elliemum. "But Baby Ellie's in a bad way. She's lost her ni-ni."

"Ni-ni Ni-ni!" cooed Baby Ellie.

"Now we know who it's precious to!" said Angelmouse.

"You're an angel, Angelmouse!" exclaimed Elliemum, kissing him.

"It's good to help people, isn't it, Quilly?" beamed Angelmouse. Suddenly, his halo returned, shining very brightly.

Then Elliemum, with a little help from Angelmouse, took Baby Ellie home for a good night's sleep.